That Summer

IN MEMORY OF MATT BARBARICS

1975–1995

IN MEMORY OF TAYLOR WELCH

1950–1990

– T. J.

For my brother, Thomas L. Moser

&

For all the courageous people who

care for terminally ill children,

with my deepest respect

and admiration

—B. M.

THAT SUMMER

by Tony Johnston

Illustrated by Barry Moser

Harcourt, Inc. ❋ San Diego   New York   London

Printed in Singapore

THAT SUMMER began like always,
with hoots and shouts, all of us running
into the sun,
freed from school,
over the porch,
over the lawn,
down the hollows.
Joey and I ran
like there was no tomorrow.

Fourth of July he took sick.
Mama said, "The child has overindulged
on pie once again."
So, gripping his belly,
Joey went to bed.

And there he stayed.

That summer moved like a dream
quavering with heat
and slow.
All of us were dream walkers
watching Joey,
Mama and Papa and Gram and I
and our dog, Spoon.

When Joey perked up, hope
fluttered inside us, like a little green
bird.
But it stilled when Joey
turned worse.

What do you do when you know
you are leaving
the world,
when your heart hurts
with grieving?
Joey was leaving.
It was clear as the rain
that stung his window
that summer.

First, he cried.

I heard him

alone

tucked into bed,

tucked into his bad dream.

So I, dream walker, brother, went in

and we cried together.

Joey was dying.

What mattered now, to me?

Nothing.

Nothing at all. Then

every

single

leaf.

Nights, when I lay awake

that summer,

a gleam of guilt glided

through my heart

like a gleam of snake

down a hole.

Joey was sick

but I was well.

That summer while Gram kept vigil,

she quilted,

and her needle flicked in and out,

a fish, slim and silver.

"How do you make a quilt?" Joey asked.

"Cut scraps into shapes

of all the things you love," Gram said,

"then join them with thread."

So in the hollows of the night

when he could not sleep

Joey pieced a quilt–

a patch with an owl because he loved

its call,

the cow he squeezed from clay

(first grade),

and his fishing pole

and a lightning bug

and a country road

and his baseball glove.

I learned a lot

that summer.

How to grin with your heart

in shreds.

How to make a bed with your brother

in it,

your brother still

as a whisper.

Each day of that summer
held small scenes–
Spoon licking Joey's face
like a big Popsicle,
Joey jutting out his jaw,
quilting.

And Joey's friends, come caroling.
In broad daylight. In July.
Boisterous, roisterous friends
caterwauling notes known only
to lonely cats,
screeching their hymn:
Joey, come out soon!
Joey pieced the scene.

Once, Joey and Gram looked up
at the stars
flung clear across forever
and Joey asked, "When
will I die?"
"Oh, my baby dear," she crooned
and held him.
"Who will care for me then?"
"God will," said Gram.

Joey quilted what he thought
was God.
It looked a lot like
Spoon.

That summer when Joey's hair fell
in clumps,
Papa shaved the rest.
When he saw his baby–bald self,
Joey cried.

Soon I came with a cap on,
pulled it off–*ta-da!*
–and I was bald too.
"*I'm* a baby," Joey told me.
I said, "*I'm* a balloon."
"We're two bald baby balloons."

Then we hugged each other,
nearly squeezed out each other's
breath.

One night that summer
amid the crickets' heartbeat song,
we gathered at home
by candlelight.
Papa and Mama and Gram and I
and Joey's friends.

The quilt was nearly done.
Just one last patch still out
left a gap
like a missing tooth.
Joey would never
finish it now
so I stitched in my masterpiece–
two bald baby balloons.

Spoon snored

beneath the frame

while we sewed a border

to bind the pieces together,

a border from Joey's

pajamas.

While we worked

no one really spoke our loss.

But from the edges of the quilt

our voices, soft warm sounds,

arose

like the purr of pigeons

in a church.

The room fell still.

I touched my smooth head.

Then into the silence, sweet and wide

as sleep,

I whispered to Joey,

Good-bye.

Requests for permission to make copies of any part of the work should be mailed to the following address:
Permissions Department, Harcourt, Inc., 6277 Sea Harbor Drive, Orlando, Florida 32887-6777.

www.harcourt.com

Library of Congress Cataloging-in-Publication Data
Johnston, Tony.
That summer/by Tony Johnston; illustrated by Barry Moser.
p.   cm.
Summary: A family, including a child who is dying, sews together a quilt of its memories and love.
[1. Quilting—Fiction.   2. Brothers—Fiction.   3. Death—Fiction.   4. Grief—Fiction.   5. Family life—Fiction.]
I. Moser, Barry, ill.   II. Title.
PZ7.J6478Tg   2002
[Fic]—dc21   2001001314
ISBN 0-15-201585-X

First edition
A C E G H F D B

The illustrations in this book were done in graphite on gray paper, heightened with white chalk,
and in transparent watercolor on paper handmade in 1982 by Simon Green at the
Barcham Green Mill in Maidstone, England, for the Royal Watercolor Society.
The display lettering was created by Tom Seibert.
The text type was set in Nofret.
Color separations by Bright Arts Ltd., Hong Kong
Printed and bound by Tien Wah Press, Singapore
This book was printed on totally chlorine-free Nymolla Matte Art paper.
Production supervision by Sandra Grebenar and Pascha Gerlinger
Designed by Barry Moser and Judythe Sieck